Coming Back

Coming Back

K.L. DENMAN

ORCA BOOK PUBLISHERS

Library and Archives Canada Cataloguing in Publication

Title: Coming back / K.L. Denman.
Names: Denman, K.L., 1957– author.

Identifiers: Canadiana (print) 20190069376 | Canadiana (ebook) 20190069384 | ISBN 9781459822665 (softcover) | ISBN 9781459824027 (PDF) | ISBN 9781459824034 (EPUB)

Classification: LCC PS867.E64 C66 2019 | DDC C813/.6—dc23

Library of Congress Control Number: 2019934030
Simultaneously published in Canada and the United States in 2019

Summary: In this work of fiction, Julie works with a therapy horse to help heal the PTSD she suffers from after a horrific car accident. (RL 2.9)

Orca Book Publishers is committed to reducing the consumption of nonrenewable resources in the making of our books. We make every effort to use materials that support a sustainable future.

Orca Book Publishers gratefully acknowledges the support for its publishing programs provided by the following agencies: the Government of Canada, the Canada Council for the Arts and the Province of British Columbia through the BC Arts Council and the Book Publishing Tax Credit.

Cover image by Shutterstock.com/ondrejsustik
Cover design by Ella Collier

ORCA BOOK PUBLISHERS
orcabook.com

Printed and bound in Canada.

22 21 20 19 • 4 3 2 1

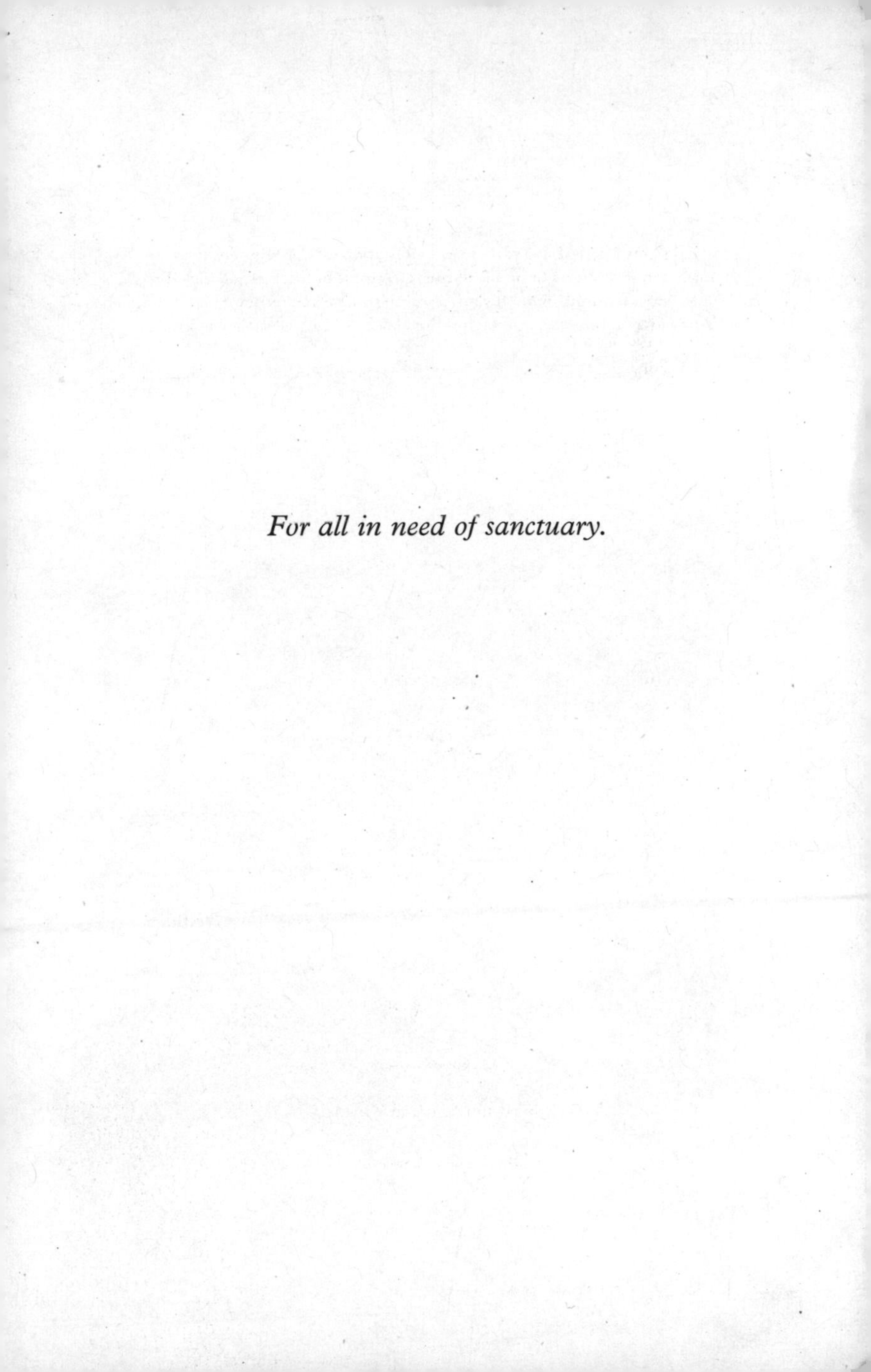

For all in need of sanctuary.

One

I'VE MADE IT to most of my appointments with Dr. Rosa Flores. But I missed the last one. I'm here now, sitting in her cozy office. It's in an old brick building with tall windows, and the decor has the feel of an old-fashioned porch. There's a pair of plump overstuffed chairs, the sort you sink into. The colors are green and cream, and the pictures on the walls are vibrant abstracts. I'm studying the flowered curtains at the window. Anything to avoid her watchful gaze.

"Has there been any change, Julie?" she asks.

She wants to know if I've been leaving my apartment. Seeing people. And the biggie: have I remembered the accident? I shake my head.

Dr. Rosa nods. "Okay. But you're here again today. And that's good. I know it takes a lot of effort."

As pathetic as that is, it's true. It takes every scrap of willpower I've got to come here. It's not that I'm afraid to leave my place. Not exactly. I just don't want to. It doesn't feel like there's any point. Nothing will change.

"Are you eating?" she asks.

I glance over and feel the warm concern she radiates. It fills the air around her. She's older, a small woman with thick black hair pulled into a soft ponytail. I shrug and reply, "Enough."

"Good. Is there anything at all you'd like to share with me?"

I despise that question. No, there is nothing I'd like to share. Not because I'm especially private, but more because there really is nothing.

When I don't reply, she asks the next question. "Are you sleeping?"

"Not really," I mutter. As in I'm still afraid to sleep. Still having the nightmares. Every night I'm chased down dark roads by a faceless man in black. He wields relentless terror.

"Julie?" Dr. Rosa leans in toward me. "I'd like you to consider a new treatment. It's not a medication. It's something that will take a strong commitment from you."

I shoot her a wary look. "I'm not trying the art or yoga classes again."

"Fine. Because this is something quite different." She pauses, watching me closely.

"I'd like to prescribe a companion animal for you. A cat perhaps. Or a dog."

I stare at her. "You want me to get a pet?" I feel something as I say this. It's a shimmery feeling I haven't had for so long, it takes me by surprise. It might be actual interest. But the shimmer swiftly dies. "My building doesn't allow pets."

Dr. Rosa raises her brows. "That may be their general rule. But by law, they have to allow an emotional-support animal."

"They do?" The shimmer of interest is back. "Are you sure?"

She grins. "They do if the animal is prescribed by a doctor. Like me."

I feel something unfamiliar happening to my face.

"Julie," she says, laughing. "You're smiling!"

It's true. But the smile fades as I resume studying the curtains. "I don't know. I've never had a pet of my own. What if I can't look after it?"

"But what if you can?" she asks. She quietly waits while I absorb that. Eventually she says, "Listen, Julie. I don't want you to make a decision yet. All I'm asking is that you think about it."

I nod. "Okay. I can do that." I don't remind her that even thinking is hard sometimes. But this? At least I *want* to think about this. That's saying something.

And I do think about it. On the drive home from Dr. Rosa's office it suddenly seems there are people walking dogs everywhere. There's a large black one with silky, wavy fur. It almost floats alongside its owner. There's a bulldog, mostly white, built low to the ground. Its thick legs are bowed, and its broad wrinkled face grins as it lumbers along the sidewalk. At a traffic light I look up and notice a calico cat watching from an apartment window.

The idea of a dog walking alongside me is tempting. And to have a cat waiting at home to cuddle and play with...that's tempting too. My family never had pets while I was growing up. My brother was allergic to them, so my only experience with animals was at friends' homes. My boyfriend...

I draw a blank there. I remember other boyfriends from the past, especially the one with the dog. Chad. We were together for two years before he dumped me. But that was before the last one, Roger. He's nothing more than a lurking shadow. Vague moments blanketed in fog. My mother says she never even saw a picture of him. I have one photo of us together, but his back is to the camera. I do remember that after Chad and I split, I met Roger online. We talked and Skyped every spare moment, and he seemed like a perfect match. Before long I moved across the country to be with him. My family and friends were shocked, but I was excited about a fresh start. I was able to get a job transfer with the law firm I worked for. Even able to put a down payment on a small condo. It wasn't long before Roger moved in with me. It seems all was well for six months—and then the car accident happened.

When I got home from the hospital, there wasn't even a stray sock to show Roger had ever been there. No note. My phone was destroyed in the accident, and my computer was scrubbed clean of messages. It was as if he had tried to erase himself, but why? Was it guilt over him being the cause of the accident? I don't know.

I only know the bare details from the police report. Roger was driving and lost control. The car rolled at high speed and was a write-off. He walked away with minor injuries. One of the nurses at the hospital said he came to visit once. And that was it.

My family and friends wanted me to move back to them right away. They said I could get therapy there. That it wasn't like I had anyone here now, not even friends. I guess I wasn't with the new office long enough to form friendships. But something in me refuses.

Part of me believes that by staying here I'll recover my missing memory. Be the person I once was. I don't want my family and friends to see what I've become. The way it is now, I can ignore calls and messages. I tell them I like it here, and besides, I own my apartment. I received a large insurance settlement from the accident, enough to pay off the condo. Enough that I don't have to work for a long time.

But they don't like that either. They've all tried to convince me I'd be better off going back to work as a paralegal. I tell them that isn't possible with my impaired concentration. My mother says, "You used to love it, Julie. It's just not like you to do *nothing*. It's been almost a year."

Yes, almost a year in limbo. Of searching through a faulty mind to find answers that refuse to come. The one friend I haven't been able to fully dodge is Kerry. She flew out to be with me after the accident—surprising since we'd parted on bad terms. Kerry hadn't held back telling me she thought it was a huge mistake for me to move to the West Coast. I hadn't held back replying that her opinion didn't matter.

But she came. And she was there when the doctors said I didn't suffer a head trauma that could account for the memory gap. Their diagnosis is post-traumatic stress disorder, and they say in time it's likely my memory will return. How much time?

I give up thinking about the past and return to the pet idea. When I get home,

I make toast and open a can of bland pea soup. I dump it into a bowl, heat it in the microwave and then sit at my computer to eat. I begin researching dog breeds, then move on to cats. I spend an hour watching funny pet videos. Some of them even make me smile.

I spend all of the next week thinking about having a pet. Hours pass as I search online, reading and looking at images. By the time I return to Dr. Rosa's office, I'm ready to give her my answer.

Two

I DON'T WAIT for Dr. Rosa to run through her usual list of check-in questions. The moment we're seated, I blurt out, "I've decided."

She knows without asking what has been decided. She grins and raises a hand, palm up. "Wonderful! I take it you're going ahead with a pet then?"

"I am."

"And?" Her brown eyes twinkle. "Shall I write the prescription for a cat or a dog?"

"Neither," I say firmly. "I'm going to get a horse."

The twinkle fades as her eyes widen, but she quickly recovers. "A horse?" She tilts her head to one side. "Do you mind my asking why?"

"The only pet I ever dreamed of having is a horse. If I'm going to do this, why not get the animal I really want?"

She studies me for a moment. "I can see why you might feel that way. But if you don't mind, I'd like to explore this choice. My first thought is practicality. Obviously you can't keep a horse in your apartment."

"I've already found a boarding stable. It's really nice and only fifteen minutes away from my place."

"Okay." She nods. "That's great. But are you willing to *go* there on a regular basis?"

I knew she'd ask this, and I'm ready for her. "I'll admit, it will be a challenge. But

I'll *have* to go, right? I mean, there's a stablc manager there. I talked to her, and she does all the chores of feeding and cleaning stalls. But she said I'd be responsible for exercising and grooming the horse. I think..." I hesitate. "No, I *know* I would go. And isn't that a win-win? Unlike a cat, *this* would make me leave the apartment."

"I don't doubt it," Dr. Rosa says. "All right, another concern. Your injuries from the accident were fairly extensive. Broken jaw, shoulder, ribs, arm and leg, correct? Horseback riding is physically demanding. Will you be up to it?"

"My physiotherapy ended a couple of months ago. The therapist said the best thing I could do from there was to exercise. See? Another win-win."

"You really have thought this through. I'm impressed. You must have great past experiences with horses."

I nod. "I rode when I was a teen and loved it. Although that was over ten years ago. But the stable manager gives lessons. I could take lessons for a while."

She smiles. "Of course. But perhaps before jumping into this, you might consider another option. There is a counselor nearby that does equine-assisted therapy. Would you like to try that first?"

"No. This is what I want. I've decided."

"Indeed. And making a decision is terrific." Dr. Rosa claps her hands. "I think this is an excellent choice. I can already see a change in you, Julie. That is wonderful. I'm so pleased."

* * *

The mare is beautiful. Exactly the horse I've imagined. Her coat is paprika red, and her mane and tail are silken auburn. She has four white stockings and a white blaze, and her muscles ripple like molten copper as she moves. The advertisement said she was five years old and a reliable trail horse. It didn't specify her breeding, but that's not important to me. I don't need a show horse.

The owner is a solid woman with a stomping walk and curly gray hair. She introduces herself as Shirley. As she leads the mare toward me, she says, "She's a dandy. And sound as a bell. Healthy as a horse, eh? Ha-ha."

I can barely take my eyes off the mare to reply. "Good. Great. Uh..." I try to recall the questions I planned to ask. I thought I'd memorized the list I found online, but it seems to be gone. Ah. "How are her feet? Is she good with the farrier?"

"She's a perfect lady. See for yourself." With that, Shirley stoops and taps the mare's ankle. Or, rather, the fetlock. I've studied horse anatomy too. Obediently the mare lifts the hoof and stands quietly. "She'll be due for a trim again in a week or so."

"Nice," I say. *What else?* "What about her teeth? Are they good?"

"Absolutely. Just had them done a month ago. And she's up to date on all her shots."

I nod. That is another question answered. "Does she have any bad habits?"

Shirley shakes her head. "No. See for yourself. She handles like a dream." Shirley steps forward and offers the mare's lead line. Gingerly I take hold, and then I'm right next to the horse. I'd forgotten how large they are up close. But I gaze into the mare's liquid brown eyes and find a sweet curiosity in them. Cautiously I reach out to run a hand along her neck. It feels like warm satin. That wonderful horse aroma fills my nostrils, and I inhale deeply.

"Go ahead," Shirley says. "Take her for a walk."

That flusters me. How does this work? Do I pull on the line? Yes. I try that, and the mare takes a half step toward me. I back up. The mare follows.

"Huh." Shirley snorts. "You might want to turn around. Don't worry—she'll follow."

I feel like an idiot. Of course that's how it's done. I turn and step forward, and sure enough, the mare stays with me. Her hooves clop loudly on the pavement, a rhythmic one-two-three-four beat. It sounds like music. When we reach the end of the paved yard, I turn and head back to Shirley. The mare follows.

"Nice, eh?" Shirley asks. "Looks like she's the perfect size for you too. Do you want to get on?"

"Um. No. Not right now. I have to take some lessons first."

Shirley squints. "Greenhorn, are ya? Hmm. Well then, do you want to watch me give her a go around the arena?"

"Sure." I watch closely as Shirley puts a Western-style saddle on the mare. Next there's a bridle with a bit that slips into the horse's mouth. It all goes quickly and smoothly. Too quickly for me to follow all the steps, but that's okay. I'll watch more online videos.

Shirley takes the horse into a large fenced area with a sandy surface and demonstrates that the mare will walk, trot, and canter. She behaves beautifully. The mare is so graceful, it's like watching a dance.

This is the one. I *know* it. My very own horse. When Shirley rides back toward the gate, I ask, "What's her name?"

"She don't really have a name. I just call her Red."

A horse with no name. That will have to change. "I'd like to take her," I say. "She's perfect."

But Shirley hesitates. "You know what, honey? I've been thinking. And I've gotta say, I'm not so sure this is the right horse for you."

I gape at her. "What? Why not?"

"Hon, she's a good little mare. But she's still young. Not really right for a novice like you."

Panic floods through me, hot and wild. "But I want her! I've looked at a few other horses, and I didn't feel a connection. This is the one!"

Shirley studies me. "How much help are you going to have?"

"Lots. The stable manager—her name's Vicki. She's a coach and everything."

"That's Vicki Hayes?" Shirley asks. "Over at the Blackwood place?"

I nod.

Shirley swings down from the horse before replying. "Okay then. I've heard Vicki has a decent reputation. And I'll guarantee the mare is sound, so you don't have to worry about a vet bill. But I'm warning you, Julie, I don't sell horses on trial. Had trouble with that in the past. Folks mess up an animal, then say they don't want it. So if things go wrong..."

"They won't," I tell her. They won't.

Three

SHIRLEY OFFERS TO trailer my beautiful mare to the boarding stable the next day. She tells me to be sure I've got cash to pay. I'll also need to have my own tack ready for her arrival. I give the mare a final pat and go from there to the tack store Shirley suggests.

The store is filled with the scent of leather and items I can't identify. Saddles are obvious, and I look at them for a while. A clerk comes over and offers help. When I tell her I've just bought a new horse and need "everything," she grabs a shopping cart.

"What breed is your horse?" she asks.

Airily I reply, "That's not important."

"Okay," says the clerk, "but you'll need to get the right size. I mean, a quarter horse is smaller than a Clydesdale, right?"

I flush. "Right. Well, she's a medium size." We're standing in front of a wall of halters. A bright green one catches my eye. "That color would look good on her."

"Perfect." The clerk takes down a green halter and puts it in the cart. An hour later I'm at the checkout with several bulging bags. Brushes, a lead line, a horse blanket, a bridle, a pair of boots for me, a hoof pick, fly spray—I don't know what some of the "basics" I bought are for, but I've got them. The total is over $1,000, and I don't even have a saddle yet.

"You have to buy a properly fitted saddle," the clerk tells me. "We have someone that goes out to barns and measures. But you need to book an appointment. Would you like to do that?"

Dazed, I nod. She makes the call while I wait. A few minutes later she asks, "Does next Monday work for you?" That's a week away, but I agree. She writes the time on a business card and hands it to me. "She charges $100 for the appointment."

By the time I go to the bank and withdraw the cash for Shirley, I'm exhausted. I haven't done so much in a single day since...since when? I don't know. I hit a drive-through for a burger and eat it on the way home. Once all the bags are hauled up to my apartment, I spread everything out in my small living room.

It's astonishing how much is required. I pick up the green halter and imagine how it will look on my horse. *My* horse! A fizzy mix of excitement and fear bubbles in my gut. What have I done? But then I picture the mare's sweet, dark eyes and take a deep breath. It's going to be fine. Better than fine. It's going to be amazing.

I wriggle my feet into my shiny new leather boots and admire their fancy stitching. The clerk said it's a good idea to break them in. I clop back and forth in the living room before settling at the computer. My plan is to research saddles, but I end up staring at the screen. I wish I'd thought to take a picture of Red.

I can't call her that. It's way too plain for such a beauty. She's more like a...Scarlett? Yes! I imagine going out to the pasture and calling, *Scarlett!* and she'll come running. On impulse I make a rare call to Kerry. For once I have something to tell her. She's surprised to hear about Scarlett but says, "That's awesome, Julie! So good to hear you sounding happy."

Happy? Yeah, maybe so. I tell her every detail, but when I describe Blackwood, I remember something. "I forgot to tell the stable! Sorry, Kerry. Got to go."

"K. Call back soon though. Let me know how it's going."

"I will." I end our call and punch in the number for the stable. "Vicki? It's Julie. Sorry I forgot to call earlier. My horse is coming tomorrow."

"Tomorrow?" she says. "That's rather short notice."

"I know. Sorry. I was just so busy with getting the tack and everything..."

She sighs. "It's okay. I'll get the stall ready in the morning. By the way, congratulations. What did you get?"

"I got a beautiful trail horse. Her name is Scarlett." I love how that sounds.

"Oh." Something in her voice sounds off. "Well. We'll see you both tomorrow then."

"Great. She's getting dropped off around eleven."

I get to the stable an hour early and find Vicki in the barn, sweeping up. She's a tall, angular woman with a crisp manner. She eyes my shiny new boots and asks, "Did you bring your tack?"

At my nod she says, "Right. I'll show you where to keep it." She leads the way to the tack room and points out a numbered saddle rack, wall hooks and a shelf to stow brushes on. "Remember, you have number twenty-two. Don't take over extra space."

Then she steps back into the center aisle and motions for me to follow. We walk almost to the end of the barn before she stops. "Your horse can have this stall." She points to a sheet of paper tacked to the wall. "This is her feeding chart. Does it look okay to you?"

My stomach clenches as I read the chart. It shows two flakes of hay to be fed *AM*, *PM* and *nighttime*. I have zero idea if that's okay, but I nod anyway.

"Good. We'll adjust it if necessary." Vicki turns to go. "I've got to get on with the chores. But I'll be around if you need me."

By the time I stow Scarlett's tack, it's almost eleven. I head to the barnyard, but no trailer has appeared yet. I pace back and forth, ignoring the sting of a blister forming on the back of my heel. The boots will need more breaking in.

It seems odd that no one else is around. When I came to look at the stable, there were people and horses everywhere. Today it's only Vicki, and all the horses are standing outside in small pens.

Which is fine. In fact, it's good. Peaceful. I draw a deep breath that catches in my throat as I see a truck and trailer pulling into the driveway. This is it. My horse is here. I shove a hand into my jacket pocket and check that the envelope of cash is there. It is. In the other pocket is a carrot, a treat for Scarlett.

The truck pulls up, tires crunching on gravel. Shirley jumps out and waves, then walks to the back of the trailer.

I'm not sure if I should join her or wait. I take a few steps forward and stop. She'd ask me to help if she needed me, right? And what could I do anyway?

The trailer door swings open, there's the sound of thudding hooves, and then Scarlett appears, backing out. Her head goes up, and she swings it from side to side, taking in her surroundings.

"Well, come on," Shirley calls. "Come get your horse."

I step forward and she says, "Wait. Don't you have a halter and lead line?"

Damn. "Yeah, sorry. I left them in the tack room. Be right back."

I turn and jog into the barn, feeling the burn of my blister. Blisters. There's one on the other heel now too.

Four

BY THE TIME I've grabbed Scarlett's halter from the tack room, Shirley has Scarlett in the barn. "It's okay," she says. "We can put her in a stall, and I'll take my halter off."

"Oh. Sure. Good." My mouth is dry.

"Which one is hers?" Shirley asks.

"Her what?"

"Her stall?" Shirley squints at me. "Unless she has a paddock. That would be even better, since she's used to being kept outside in a herd."

"Oh. I didn't know that." There's a lot I don't know. "Um...Vicki only showed me her stall. It's this way." I point, then start limping toward the end of the barn. Scarlett's hooves clop along behind me as Shirley follows. The rhythmic sound calms me. It's going to be okay. I find the right stall and open the door.

Shirley leads Scarlett inside, removes her halter and steps back out. Scarlett circles the space, then thrusts her head through the open top half of the door. I reach out to stroke her neck. But she raises her head and belts out a whinny. In my ear, it's louder than a trumpet blast.

I jump, Scarlett startles backward, and Shirley chuckles. "Scared ya, eh?"

My heart is racing, and I can't speak. I manage a nod as I recognize that I've been triggered. I use one of the grounding skills Dr. Rosa taught. In my head, I start naming things. *Horse. Stall. Wood. Hoof. Mane. Tail.* It's meant to bring me back into the moment. I glue my eyes on Scarlett. She's circling the stall again, and then she stops to paw at the floor.

"It's going to take her a bit to settle in," Shirley says. "Might want to take her out for a walk."

"Now?" I croak.

Shirley shrugs. "Soon. It'll help her get used to the place."

"Okay."

Vicki appears, striding toward us. "Hi there." She nods at Shirley. "I'm Vicki Hayes, the manager here. How are you?"

"Can't complain, but sometimes I still do," Shirley says. "How about you?"

"I'm well, thank you," Vicki replies. "Let's have a look at this mare." She peers into the stall. "Oh. What have we here?"

"A nice little horse. Has a good mind." Shirley glances at me. "Have you got the money on you?"

The money. My mind goes blank. Where is it? My purse is in the car. I open my mouth to say *I'll go get it*, then remember and reach into my pocket. "Here you go."

Shirley takes the envelope and hands me a receipt. "Thanks." She gazes at Scarlett and sighs. "Take care of Red, eh? Send me a picture sometime."

I nod, and both of the women walk away. I turn to Scarlett. She's watching Shirley go. She snorts, and then another whinny rings out. And another. She circles the stall, her nostrils flaring wide.

"Hey," I murmur. "It's okay. Shhhh."

She continues pacing, and I feel helpless. Clearly she's upset, but I have no idea how to calm her. I should know how to do that. I reach out again to stroke her, but my hand barely connects as she slips by. I jam my hands into my pockets and find the carrot. I lay it flat on my palm and offer it to Scarlett.

"Here. Look what I brought you."

Scarlett sniffs at the carrot and knocks it to the ground. She keeps going around and around the stall. It suddenly seems far too small for her, and I want to get her out of there. Shirley said I should take her for a walk.

Her halter still dangles from my arm. All I need to do is slip into the stall and put it on. But how can I go in with her in constant motion? People must do it all the time. It should be easy. I examine the halter, refreshing my memory about how it goes on. Take a deep breath. Unlatch the stall door. Slide it open, just enough to squeeze through.

Scarlett stops pacing and looks at me. For all of one second. Then she snorts and turns away. "Hey. Hey girl. Whoa."

The *whoa* works. Scarlett halts. Heart pounding, I step toward her. I can do this.

I *have* to do this. I reach out and stroke her neck. It's hot. And she's trembling. She feels like me.

I raise the halter. "It's okay. I'm going to get you out of here. I just have to put this part around your nose..." Easier said than done. I'm all thumbs, fumbling. The round part goes on, but somehow the strap part needs to go behind her ears. I pull the nose part off and step back to reexamine the halter.

Scarlett goes for the open door. She thrusts her head through and pushes forward with her shoulders.

"No! Wait! Stop!"

The door slides wide open, and she's gone. Her hoofbeats echo almost as loudly as my heartbeat as she bolts down the aisle.

Five

THE PANIC IS a physical assault. My knees buckle, and I sag against the wall. Struggle to breathe. But a vision arises of Scarlett racing out of the barn, down the driveway... onto the road. I push myself upright and start to run.

Not run. Hobble-jog. The blisters on my heels are on fire. I grit my teeth and keep going.

There's a shout outside, and then Shirley's distant voice hollers, "Whoa, Red! Whoa!"

Shirley's still here! Will Scarlett listen? I emerge from the barn to see Shirley's truck and trailer stopped at the end of the driveway. And she has Scarlett. Sort of. It looks like she's holding her by the mane.

"Bring me a halter!" she yells.

The halter is still on my arm, and I force myself to move faster. But Vicki is there too, and she comes up beside me. "Slow down. You don't want to spook her."

I slow to a walk and hobble toward Shirley. The look on her face is grim, but she doesn't say a word. Not until I hand her the halter and she has it secured on Scarlett. Then: "What the hell happened?"

I'm too numb to speak. I just shake my head.

"You hurt?" Shirley asks.

Again I shake my head.

Vicki looks at Shirley. "I thought you said this horse has a good mind. Huh. Typical high-strung chestnut mare, I'd say."

"That's bullcrap! She's a good horse." Shirley glares at Vicki. "And I've got a mind to take her back right now."

I find my voice. "No. Please. It was my fault. I was trying to put the halter on and—"

"And you didn't." Shirley shakes her head. "How much of a greenhorn are you?"

"It's been a while," I mutter.

"Well, it ain't safe for you or the horse if you don't know what you're doing." She turns back to Vicki. "I'm not leaving this horse here unless you can guarantee you'll be supervising. *Everything*."

Vicki's face takes on a sour look. "Well, this isn't the horse *I* would have chosen for her. But she will be getting lessons."

I might as well be invisible. The women keep talking.

Shirley snorts. "Riding lessons aren't going to cut it. Julie needs square-one basics.

You going to give her that too?"

Vicki hesitates. "I don't have time for that. But I can probably get one of the girls here to help her out." She glances at me. "There are a few girls who do chores in the afternoon. I'm sure one of them will do it. If you pay them."

My face is hot with embarrassment. "Sure."

Shirley still looks grim, but she hands Vicki the lead line. "Fine. I'm in the business of training and selling horses. But that don't mean I don't care about 'em. Horses deserve someone who knows what they're doing."

My embarrassment magnifies to shame. Maybe I don't deserve Scarlett. I should tell Shirley to take her back. But I can't form the words, and Vicki is leading Scarlett away. Toward a pen this time. I avoid Shirley's gaze and keep my eyes on Scarlett.

Shirley turns away, then stops. "Listen,

Julie. I know all about loving horses. But I also know some women use 'em as crutches. And they've got all these airy-fairy notions about galloping along some beach." She waves her hands. "Wind blowing in their hair. It's all about a dream. And a horse can take you there—if you put them first. You see?"

When I don't answer, she goes on. "I'm not sayin' this won't work out. I hope it does. Even though I can see you've got some issues. Not going to ask about that. Listen...I don't usually do this. But if you run into problems, you call me. All right?"

I swallow hard and nod. "Thanks."

"Now go bandage those blisters." She winks and climbs into her truck.

I limp back up the driveway. I'm spent, mentally and physically, but I make my way toward the pen holding Scarlett.

Vicki hangs the mare's halter on a peg

and turns to me. "That woman. Typical know-it-all."

She looks like she expects an answer. I manage, "Yeah."

She points at Scarlett. "We'll leave her here for now. There's some hay for her. We'll just have to see how she gets along with the neighbors." The horses penned on either side of Scarlett are clearly curious. Their necks are stretched over the fence rails, noses sniffing.

"Okay. Should I, uh, maybe watch for a while?"

"Could do," Vicki says. "Are you planning to hang around? The girls get here after school, around three thirty."

"Oh. Well, I might go home for a bit. Then come back."

"Okay." She nods toward the horses. "I think they'll get along fine. But let me know if there's a problem."

Once again I'm left alone with Scarlett. I sink to the ground in front of the pen and pull off my boots. My socks are stuck to my heels, so I leave them on. I look at Scarlett. She seems better now. She snorts at the other horses, but she doesn't whinny. She takes a mouthful of hay, and I watch her eat.

"Sorry," I murmur. "I have a lot to learn. But I'll take care of you. Okay? I will."

It might be my imagination, but I feel like she's listening. "You really scared me. And Shirley was right, you know. I do have issues. But I'm not going to let that hurt you. I promise. It'll be fine. You'll see. It will."

Am I trying to convince her? Or myself?

The weariness I feel is suddenly so heavy, I wonder if I can stand. I manage it, remember to pick up my boots and walk in sock feet to my car.

Six

THE REPETITIVE TONE comes from far away. It's annoying. I want it to stop, and it does. Then it starts again. I fight the shift from murky sleep, but I lose. Someone is calling, and they aren't giving up.

The caller ID shows Vicki's name. I just left the barn. Why would she be calling? I answer, "Hello?"

"Julie? I thought you were planning to come back. I have Alexa here waiting for you."

"Who?"

Impatience enters Vicki's tone. "Alexa. She's one of the barn girls. She agreed to coach you on some basics."

"Oh. Uh. What time is it?"

Vicki sighs. "It's almost six. Listen, let's forget it for today. She has to leave soon. But do you want to plan for tomorrow?"

I'm fully awake now, blinking at the clock on my nightstand. How is it six? I got home at one. I must have slept all afternoon.

"Julie?"

"Yeah. Sorry. That sounds good. Tomorrow, I mean. At six?"

"No. Alexa has to leave here by six." Vicki pauses. "Are you okay?"

"Yes. I'm fine. Just...um." I clear my throat. "So I should be there at three thirty?"

"Sure. And I told her you'd pay twenty dollars per session for her help."

"Okay," I reply. "How is Scarlett?"

"She's fine." The impatience is back in Vicki's voice. "I've got to go. We'll see you tomorrow then?"

"Yes. Thanks."

Vicki says no problem and hangs up. No problem. Except for me. I was just going to lie down for a moment, and I'd still be sleeping if she hadn't called. What is wrong with me? Right. PTSD. But making up for sleepless nights by passing out during the day hasn't happened for a while.

I roll off the bed and wince as I stand. The blisters. My dirty socks are still on my feet. I give one of them a tug, but it's stuck fast. Maybe I'll have to shower with them on. That works to get the socks off. I toss them in the garbage, then apply ointment and bandages. Kick the boots.

My usual bowl of canned soup is tasteless. I eat it anyway and consider going back to the barn. Just to check on Scarlett. I need to see for myself that she's okay. Is she still outside? In the stall? I know nothing about the routine at the barn. But if I go back now, will that seem weird? I'm tempted to call Vicki, but she didn't sound like she had time to talk.

There are thousands of online how-to videos on horse care. As I watch, my confusion grows. There is so much conflicting information. When I rode horses with my friend as a teen, it all seemed so easy. Pure joy. Like most of life was back then. Maybe my memory is selective, but I know I was a completely different person. I consider reactivating my social media account, so I can see that.

But no, the last time I logged in, it felt weirdly threatening. Also depressing. There was a mix of disturbing world news and old friends leading wonderful, full lives. They were likely posting only the good times, but it was a stark contrast to my dull world. When I mentioned it to Dr. Rosa, she said I might try to engage rather than observe, but I couldn't.

What made me think about that? Right. The friend I used to ride with. I'd call her for advice right now if we hadn't lost touch.

Lost touch. On so many levels. But today when I touched Scarlett, I *felt* her. In that moment a recognition happened. True, what I recognized wasn't joy—it was fear. But it was real.

I don't want her to be afraid. I can't let that happen. I switch off the computer and pick up my journal. The last thing I wrote in there yesterday was a series of quotes about horses. I find one by Buck Brannaman: *The horse is a mirror to your soul. Sometimes you might not like what you see. Sometimes you will.*

I didn't like what I found in Scarlett

today. But tomorrow will be better. I'll make it better.

* * *

Alexa is about fourteen, a pudgy blonde with tight pants and a smirk. "Hey," she says.

"Hey." I've got my tote full of brushes and am eager to groom Scarlett. "Ready to help me get her out of the pen?"

"The pen?" Alexa wrinkles her nose. "Do you mean the paddock?"

"I guess."

"Yeah." She rolls her eyes. "We call them paddocks."

"Okay."

"So, yeah. Like, just leave the brushes there and we'll go get your horse." She leads the way, and I follow. When we reach Scarlett's *paddock*, I join Alexa at the gate. I'm eager to touch Scarlett again, to feel that connection.

Alexa holds up a hand. "Uh. Maybe you should wait here." She points at my feet. I'm wearing a comfy pair of old sneakers. Thick bandages protect my raw heels.

"So FYI," Alexa says, "you should wear proper footwear around horses. Like, boots."

I grimace. "Yeah. I get that. But I'm not riding today, just grooming."

"Still. You know horses can step on your feet, right? And they're really heavy, so it totally hurts? So probably I should just go in and get her."

I sigh. "Thanks. But Alexa? *I* want to put the halter on Scarlett."

"Oh." Alexa's smirk turns into a frown. "But Vicki told me you don't know how."

I feel my jaw clenching. "I had a problem yesterday, and that's why you're here. But really, I just need you for backup." When her frown becomes a scowl, I add, "Don't get me wrong. I appreciate your help."

She shrugs. "Okay. Whatever. Go ahead."

I open the gate and approach Scarlett, halter in hand. She stands quietly.

"Julie?" Alexa says. "You should've, like, closed the gate behind you."

I halt. "Oh. Right. I thought you were coming in with me."

She mutters, "Oh my god," under her breath. Then, "Fine. I'll come in."

Sudden heat blazes in my gut, but I simply say, "Thank you." Could the girl be any more arrogant? I inhale, exhale and approach Scarlett again. I'm determined to put the halter on correctly. I must have watched the how-to video ten times last night. And this time, it goes smoothly. Perfectly. I stroke Scarlett's silky neck, and the heat fades to a warm glow.

"Okay," Alexa says. "Let's go."

I follow her back to the barn, basking in the joy of leading my very own horse. I turn my head to admire Scarlett. Her copper coat glistens in the sun.

There are quite a few other people around the barn now, and one says hi as we pass by. The others are mostly teens, clustered in chatty groups. They ignore us. When Alexa reaches a space off the center aisle, she stops. "So here's the grooming rack. You can bring her in here."

The space is about the size of a stall, but there's no door. I lead Scarlett in, and she snorts. Alexa says, "So turn her around. Then hook her up to the cross ties."

Cross ties? I turn around and Scarlett follows, but when I put a hand on her shoulder, it feels tense. "Um. Okay. Can you show me how the cross ties work?"

Alexa's smirk is back. "It's easy." She reaches for a bungee type cord hanging from the side wall. "Just clip this on her halter here." She demonstrates. "And then do the same on the other side." She stands back and crosses her arms. Clearly, I'm expected to do the other side.

"Okay." I step around Scarlett and reach for the cord. But the clip on the end doesn't have a visible opening. "How does this work?"

Alexa steps up. "Simple. Just push it onto the ring on her halter. See?" She snaps the clip on.

Scarlett snorts again and shuffles sideways. She's held by the cords on either side, now strung across the front of the opening.

"Huh," Alexa says. "Hasn't she been in cross ties before?"

"I don't know," I mutter.

"Hope she isn't going to be an idiot about it."

Scarlett does seem uneasy. I run a hand along her neck and again feel that deep tremor. "It's okay," I murmur.

Alexa suddenly yells, "Stand!"

Scarlett startles and backs away. The cords holding her stretch tight, and she leaps forward. She stops short just in front of Alexa, nostrils flaring. “Jeez,” Alexa says. “She’s kind of stupid.”

It’s a slap in the face, as though she said *I’m* stupid. “Excuse me?”

Alexa shrugs. “She should know what *stand* means.”

Another teen saunters up beside Alexa. “She really should,” the girl says.

“So anyway.” Alexa pulls out a phone and glances at it. “I’ve got some other chores, and I need to see my horse. You’re all good, right?”

I nod. I just want them to go.

But Alexa lingers. “It’s, like, twenty bucks?”

I dig the twenty out of my pocket and hand it to her.

The girls leave, heads together, whispering.

I dislike the confines of the space as much as Scarlett does and take a long, shaky breath. But I still want to groom her. Except I left the brush tote down the aisle, in front of her stall. Is it okay to leave Scarlett here while I go get it?

And then I sense another presence. I look up to find the older teen, the one that said hi. Hesitantly she asks, "Is everything all right?"

I shake my head. "I left the brushes down there." I point.

"I'll grab them for you." Seconds later she's back with the tote. "I'm Deepa. What's your horse's name?"

"Scarlett."

Deepa nods. "She's beautiful."

The flush I feel this time is pleasant. "Thanks."

"And just in case you want to know, you don't have to groom in the cross ties.

I don't like them. I use the hitching rail outside if it's nice out. Or I stay in the stall if it's not."

Seven

OVER THE NEXT few days, I find a routine. I go in the morning to groom Scarlett—when only Vicki is around. She waves in passing as I bring the brushes out to the hitching rail. When I'm done grooming, I lead Scarlett to a patch of grass beside the driveway and let her graze. Even on the weekend, most of the teens don't show up until eleven. Which is when I leave.

I return in the evening to bring Scarlett into her stall. It's then that I must encounter the other boarders, but I do it. For Scarlett. I ignore all of them except Deepa. We exchange hellos, and that's about it. When Vicki asks how it's going with Alexa's help, I tell her once was enough. I'm fine.

And I am. My only worry is that Scarlett isn't getting any exercise. I'm getting exercise, walking and grooming her. Brushing her becomes the favorite part of my day. Combing her mane and tail to silky perfection is satisfying. I love the way her eyelids droop shut when the softest brush strokes her nose. And somehow the large warmth of her body seems to absorb all my anxiety. My sleep improves, and I have an appetite again too.

When I'm not with her, I keep watching online videos, keep reading. I clean my boots and wear them around the apartment. And when Monday arrives, I'm ready for the saddle-fitting appointment. I'm excited.

Once we have the saddle, I can begin riding lessons.

Darla arrives to do the fitting. She asks me to bring Scarlett out to the barnyard, near her van. She starts taking measurements. Then she lays a folded white sheet over Scarlett and brings out a saddle. "I brought along a few to try," she says. She settles the saddle on Scarlett's back and examines the fit. Shakes her head. "She'll need a wider size."

Darla brings out another saddle to try and again isn't satisfied. "This one's too wide. Almost sitting on her withers." The third one seems to be the charm. "Let's cinch it up and move her around some."

I watch closely as she cinches the saddle and Scarlett stands perfectly still. "Nice little mare you've got here. Good manners."

"Thanks," I say.

"Who's your trainer?"

"I don't really have one. But she was trained by Shirley Henderson."

"Oh, nice. Shirley's one of the best."

I consider that. Shirley almost took Scarlett back, and the things she said hurt. But Scarlett *does* have good manners. There hasn't been a single problem after that first day—and that problem was my fault. "Good to know," I say.

"Now," Darla says, "why don't you get up there for a minute?"

"What?"

"Get on your horse and ride her around some. Then we'll check the sheet for pressure marks."

"Oh." I swallow hard. "I haven't actually ridden her yet."

Darla squints at me. "What? Why not?"

"No saddle."

Darla looks puzzled. "Well, there's one on her now."

I nod. There is. And why not? It's not as if I've never done it. I grasp the saddle, place my foot in the stirrup and...I'm up! I can't suppress the ridiculous grin stretching across my face.

Until Darla says, "Nice that she'll go in a halter for you. But don't you at least want the line to steer?"

The line. I'm sitting on Scarlett with no way to control her. What was I thinking?

"Here," Darla says. She hands me the middle section of the lead rope. Then she loops the rest of the line over Scarlett's neck and ties it to the halter. "That should do."

When Shirley rode Scarlett, she put a bridle on her, with a bit in Scarlett's mouth. I have no idea if I can control her with only a halter. But I decide to try. I tug on the line in my left hand to aim Scarlett's head away from Darla. Then I give Scarlett a little kick.

She flinches slightly and immediately

starts walking down the driveway. My breath catches in my throat as my body recognizes the movement. This. I know this! I look ahead, through her ears, reach down and stroke her neck. Wow. I'm riding! We keep walking down the driveway, and I feel like I could go forever.

"Okay," Darla calls. "It's looking good. Do you want come back this way at a trot?"

A trot? Am I ready for that? I hesitate and turn my head to look back. It suddenly seems like a long way. We've reached the patch of grass where I take Scarlett to graze, and she stops. I have to decide. She drops her head to the grass and starts munching.

"Not now, Scarlett." I tug on the line and pull her head back up. She drops it again. I pull up again, harder, and turn her head back toward the barn. I give her another kick, firmer this time.

And just like that, we're trotting. I bounce

in the saddle and start slipping to one side. Scarlett shifts in the direction of my lean. I right myself, and she adjusts course again. Then I lose my grip on the lead rope and slip to the other side. She angles that way. The looped lead rope flaps loosely on her neck, and I struggle to grasp it. Reel it in.

We're almost back to Darla's van when I get a grip (literally) and pull back on the line. Scarlett stops.

"Well," Darla says with a chuckle, "that wasn't exactly what I meant about moving her around. But it'll work. You want to get down now so I can check?"

I smile feebly and slide awkwardly to the ground. Darla hands me the lead line and unsaddles Scarlett. She pulls the white sheet off and flips it over. "See here?" She points to some dirty smudges on the sheet. "The dirt imprints show us the pressure points from the saddle."

I peer at the sheet. One pair of marks seems slightly more pronounced than the others. "So there was more pressure here?"

"Exactly. But that's not bad at all. If the saddle was poorly fitted, those marks would be a lot darker. I'd say this saddle will do just fine."

I look at the saddle. The leather is warm amber, and the tooling pattern around the edges is beautiful. "Nice."

"Yeah. It's not a fancy show saddle with silver and all." Darla runs a hand over the seat. "But it has a bit of padding for the rider, and it's quality leather. None of that synthetic crap."

"How much is it?" I ask.

"This one is $2,400. You can call into the store with a credit card if you want me to leave it with you. And I can throw in a saddle pad and girth too."

"Um. Wow. I didn't expect it to be quite

that much." I hesitate. "Is there anything for a lower price?"

Darla shrugs. "There is. But it might not fit so well. You don't want to get something that hurts the horse. Neither of you will be happy with that."

"No, no. Of course not. Okay. Let me just grab my card from the car."

Darla nods. "And my fee for the fitting is $100. I prefer cash, if you have it."

I do have it. But that was meant for the farrier who is coming tomorrow to trim Scarlett's hooves. I'll have to make another trip to the bank machine.

Darla is packing to go when Vicki shows up. She looks at the new saddle sitting on the rail and does a double take. "You bought a *Western* saddle?"

I blink at her. "Um. Yeah."

"But...this is an English barn. I teach dressage here. Not *Western* riding."

Darla gets behind the wheel of her van and rolls down the window. "I understood Julie was looking to trail ride."

I nod. "That's right. And Scarlett was trained in a Western saddle."

Darla grins at Vicki. "It shouldn't be a problem for the basics. The main difference is reining. A decent coach can teach both."

Vicki's eyes narrow. "Of course," she says thinly.

Eight

I GO HOME teetering on the edge of that heavy exhaustion I loathe. My bed beckons, but I can't trust it to let me sleep. This feels like a prime nightmare night. I flop onto my couch and listen to a phone message from Dr. Rosa. "Hi, Julie. You missed your appointment today. Hope that just means you've been having so much fun with your new horse that you forgot to come in. Please give me a call."

Having so much fun with my new horse.

Truthfully, very little of it has been fun. When I'm alone with Scarlett, it's wonderful. I fall more in love with her every day. And the taste of riding, clumsy as it was, was fabulous. But the rest? There's a constant sensation of being off balance. Of being inferior. Of being judged and found wanting.

I picture the tack room. When I placed my new saddle in the tack room, it was an oddity. Far down in the corner were two dusty old Western saddles. The rest were all English style. Why hadn't I noticed this before? And instead of ignoring the other boarders, I looked at them. All were wearing fitted breeches with tall black boots. I overheard snickers from the tack room when the girls went in. Alexa didn't bother to conceal her smirk when she drawled, "Nice saddle, Julie."

Meh. What difference does style make? It's about Scarlett, about getting out of the apartment. About not suffocating. About connecting with another living being.

And then my phone rings. It's Vicki. "Julie? You should have spoken to me before buying that saddle. First you bought the wrong type of horse. Now you've got the wrong saddle. When you came to ask about boarding at Blackwood, I thought you understood that this is a dressage barn. If I'd known what you were up to...well, you could have consulted me about the type of horse to buy. It's not easy to make it in this business, and I'm trying to build a reputation. I want my students showing and winning ribbons. Not wasting my time."

I can't speak.

"Julie? I'm just trying to be upfront with you. I have space in the barn for now, but unless you want to sell her and change horses..."

"No."

"No?" She finally pauses. "You could at least consider it. It's not like you've had her for long. I have to say, I was looking forward to having a more mature student. Someone who would take this seriously."

There's a sudden rage inside me, and my brain explodes with words. *You mean someone who furthers your agenda? You just want to manipulate me. You and your snotty little brat helpers. You're all about image. You never told me this shit about dressage when I came. You have five empty stalls there. If you're such a bigshot coach, why is that? You're just a bully. All you want are minions. And my money. So you can count me out!*

But not one of those words comes out of my mouth.

I hear Vicki heave a sigh. "All right. We'll figure it out. I was certified to coach Western riding—years ago. The basics *are* similar, but we'll have to do private lessons.

None of my other students will be interested. It's sixty dollars for each forty-minute lesson. I'd say we should do three a week."

"Okay."

"We can start tomorrow." There's a rustling of paper and she adds, "One o'clock?"

"Sure."

"I'll meet you in the arena. Have Scarlett tacked up and ready to go."

We end the call with Vicki's words echoing in my head. *Have Scarlett tacked up.* Meaning I'll have to put the saddle and bridle on myself. My jaw clenches as I force myself to the computer and resume watching how-to videos. I can do this. I *want* to do this. It *will* work out.

I arrive at the barn at eleven. That will allow plenty of time to groom Scarlett and practice putting on her tack. But waiting at the side door of the barn is the farrier. He's wearing a leather apron, and his tools are set up on the tailgate of his pickup. He's a muscular guy with tattoos along his arm and a toothy grin. "Hey. You must be Julie?"

I nod.

He sticks out a callused hand, and I gingerly place mine in his. "Yeah. And you're Bill, right?"

"Yup. Glad you showed up. But in future, I'd appreciate you having the horse ready for me."

"Right. Sorry about that." There is no way I want to tell him I completely forgot the appointment. "I'll just go get her."

"Thanks," Bill says. "I'll be waiting."

I jog down to Scarlett's paddock and on the way remember that I don't have cash for Bill. I gave it to Darla. Now what? I slip the halter on Scarlett and lead her up to the barn. Maybe he'll take a credit card? I ask him that.

"You've gotta be kidding. Didn't Vicki tell you it's check or cash only?"

Glumly I nod. "Yes. But I don't carry checks and I forgot to stop at the bank."

He shakes his head. "Listen, I've got the whole day booked, so I can't wait around. If I knew you as a regular, I'd just say I'll get it next time. But as it is..."

He must see something in my face, because he relents. "How about this? I'll see if your horse is going to behave. And if you're not necessary to keep her in line, you can go to the bank while I work."

"Okay. Thank you! I just bought her from Shirley, and she said Scarlett's great with her feet."

"That's Shirley Henderson?" He nods. "I've worked on her horses before. And if this one's like her others, we should be fine." He directs me to stand with Scarlett in the open doorway and picks up a front foot. "No shoes. You want to keep her barefoot?" he asks.

For once, I'm prepared. I've read about this. "I think that's fine. We aren't going on any trails yet. And her hooves look healthy. No cracks or anything."

"Okay, you got it." He pulls a pair of long-handled clippers from a loop on his apron and bends to pick up Scarlett's front hoof. "Uh...would you mind giving me some room here, Julie? It works better if you stand on the other side of her head."

I flush and move aside, and he starts trimming the rim of Scarlett's hoof. She stands perfectly calm and still. He pauses and says, "Looks like we're good. Let's just put her in the cross ties here, and you can go."

The cross ties again. Scarlett hasn't been in them since that first day. "She's not used to them. But when I tie her to the rail, she's fine."

"Okay," Bill says. "We'll try the rail. But if that doesn't work, the only way *I'm* working is if Vicki will cover this for you.

Either she holds your horse, or she pays so you can. Sorry, but I've been burned too many times by deadbeat clients. Can't do business like that."

As I lead Scarlett to the rail, I whisper to her, "Please, Scarlett. Just behave. Please."

And she does. She stands quietly at the rail, and I go to the bank. I'm ridiculously proud of also remembering to get my lesson money. Ridiculous, because there was a time when remembering such a simple task would have been automatic. I'm back just as Bill finishes filing the last hoof. He chats for a bit as he packs up his tools. By the time he goes, it's well past noon. I still need to groom Scarlett. Practice getting the saddle and bridle on. And I really need to pee.

I lead Scarlett into her stall and race to the washroom. The toilet paper has run out, and for an awful moment I think I'm going to cry. I'm saved by a tissue in my pocket.

Nine

THE ARENA IS a large, covered rectangle with sandy ground. Neither Scarlett nor I have gone in before, but she's fine with it. She looks around curiously as I scrub the back of my sleeve across my brow. I'm sweating from the repeated attempts to get her saddle in place, but I did it.

The bridle though. I'm carrying it over my shoulder. I'll need Vicki's help for that. I did get it on once, but the fit was all wrong. There are buckles to adjust it, but it was too much. Asking for help again with the basics isn't something I want to do, but I'll have to.

Vicki strides in and eyes us. "You're not ready?"

"No. The bridle doesn't fit." I almost cringe, dreading another shot of criticism.

But she merely says, "Hmm. Let's have a look." She takes the bridle and holds it up alongside Scarlett's head. "It's too long."

"Yes. The bit was practically hanging out of her mouth."

Vicki adjusts some buckles and says, "Let's try this." I watch closely. She works fast, removing Scarlett's halter and slipping on the bridle. She leaves the bridle on to make another adjustment and says, "That's perfect."

"Thanks."

She waves a hand. "No worries. Now, where's your helmet?"

"What?"

"Your helmet." Vicki frowns. "No one can ride here without one. It's not safe."

I don't have a helmet. I look helplessly at Vicki, and she sighs. "I've got some spares, so you can borrow one for today. But you're going to need your own."

She leaves and returns a few minutes later with a black helmet. "In case you're wondering, even most Western riders are wearing them now." She hands it to me. "Try it on."

I plunk the helmet onto my sweaty head, and it seems to fit. Except for the chin strap. Vicki instructs me to tighten it and then glances at her watch. "All this has wasted lesson time. I hope you can see why I wanted you ready at one o'clock sharp?"

I'm tempted to say, "Yes sir," but I only nod. She moves back and says, "All right then. Take your reins and mount up."

A deep breath in. Exhale. I grasp the reins and swing up into the saddle. I settle into the seat and once again am flooded with delight.

"That needs work," Vicki says. "And you didn't check your saddle girth. Plus your stirrups are too long."

She tells me to get off and check the girth. It feels snug enough to me, but Vicki tightens it. Then she shows me how to hold my arm along the length of the stirrup leather to check for the right length. I wonder why she didn't do this before. It almost feels like she was expecting my mistakes. Finally she says, "Okay. Mount up again."

Then she talks me through mounting correctly. I just thought it was a matter of sticking my foot in the stirrup and pulling myself up. But no. There is a right way and a wrong way. She gives reasons as we go, and it all makes sense. I practice it about ten times.

At last she lets me stay in the saddle. "Okay, just take her at a walk toward C."

See? I glance at Vicki. "Where?"

She points toward the far end of the arena. I notice a large letter *C* placed on the wall. There are other letters too, spaced all around the arena.

We're already facing in that direction, so I tap my heels to Scarlett. She flinches and starts walking forward.

"Julie. Your horse doesn't appear to need a *kick*. You can simply squeeze your legs."

The horse I rode as a teen always needed a kick to go, but I suspect Vicki is right. Scarlett is a dream to ride. We walk on, and as we near the wall, Vicki calls, "Track left to H."

"Track left?"

"Turn left. Then keep going straight on the long side."

I turn Scarlett as instructed and ride

beside the wall. Vicki stays quiet, but I feel her scrutiny. When we near the other end, she says, "Just keep going around."

We do. We circle the entire arena twice before Vicki finally calls, "Now bring her back to center and halt."

Once we're there, she says, "You don't have a *terrible* seat. Your back is straight, and your hands are okay. However..."

And now she's talking. On and on about my poor balance. Leg position. My elbows. Even my chin. I try to follow all she says, but it's like I suddenly have too many body parts. Obviously, I'm a lousy rider.

Vicki must notice that my eyes have glazed over. "As you can see, we have a lot to work on. But that's enough for now."

Enough? I barely got to ride. "Can I just go around a few more times?"

She frowns. "I have another student coming in at two." She glances at her watch.

"That's in ten minutes. You should check the schedule posted outside my office. It shows free times for the arena. But I doubt you should be riding alone yet."

Screw that! I think it. But I don't say it.

Over the next month a new pattern emerges. I continue to go twice daily to see Scarlett. Her ears perk up when she sees me, and she often greets me with a glad whinny. She's eager to get out of the small paddock or stall. When I groom her, I find the places where she loves to be scratched. She leans into my hands and daintily takes the carrots I offer as treats.

When I lead her out for grass, her silent company is peaceful. She's simply with me and I'm with her. No judgment. We wander farther, out along the road. I drift with her, notice how her ears tilt toward sounds, including my voice. She's hyperaware of the world around us. Like I am with PTSD, always on alert. I read about how for horses, as prey animals, this is about survival. That's how it feels to me too.

Sometimes she gets a bit bossy, pulling me in the direction she wants. Other times she resists going back to her stall. I swear she makes faces, clenching her jaw or tensing her brows. I feel guilty enclosing her in the small spaces, but mostly it's perfect.

Kerry calls, and I tell her how much I'm enjoying Scarlett's company. I don't tell her the riding lessons are completely different. Three times a week I go into the arena and listen to Vicki tell me all I do wrong. With each passing lesson, my confidence in my ability shrinks. I can't concentrate. Or I get so rattled I make mistakes that even I recognize. I jerk on the reins. I kick Scarlett too hard. I try correcting my leg position and lose my balance. I fall off more than once. The bruises to my shaky ego are worse than the ones on my body. Worst of all is how my anxiety affects Scarlett—she's tense and jittery too.

I tell Vicki I'd like to take lessons on the trail. Just have some fun rides. She tells me there aren't any nearby trails. We'd have to load the horses onto a trailer and haul them somewhere. She doesn't have time for that.

A day comes when I decide I must practice on my own. No one is around when I saddle Scarlett and lead her out to the pasture. I don't want to ride in the arena, where I might be seen. So far Vicki hasn't turned any horses out onto the grass. It's an open field, surrounded by trees and shrubs. Perfect.

I mount up. Scarlett stands still, head high, gazing at the open space. Then she whinnies. An answer comes from one of the paddocks. She swivels her head that way and makes for the gate. My heart starts pounding.

"No. Whoa." I pull back on the reins, and she halts. "We're going to ride around the pasture, okay?" I turn her to face the open field. This is it. I nudge her with my heels. She starts walking, head swinging from side to side as she looks around.

"Okay," I say. "That's fine. You take a look." I stroke her neck, hoping to calm both of us. She drops her head to the grass and starts eating.

I haul up on the reins. "No. We're not here to graze." My kick is sharper than intended.

She explodes into a gallop. We career down the field. In the first seconds, my mind is utterly blank. And then I'm gasping with panic. "No!" I scream. I'm bouncing on her back, arms and legs flapping. "Stop!"

Scarlett keeps going. If anything, her speed increases. I struggle to gather the reins but only manage to pull up on one. When she swerves left in response, my body goes right. For a moment it feels as though I'm hanging in midair. And then I hit the ground—hard. I land on my butt and tumble sideways into a roll.

It's as if I've been thrown through space and time. I'm back in the car accident, rolling, snapping, breaking into pieces. Blackness swamps me.

Ten

I DON'T LOSE consciousness. Not really. It was a flashback, the most intense I've had. I lie in the grass and fight to clear it. And then I fight to reclaim it. Because there was something new in that memory. A face. Roger's face? Distorted with...pain? It must be. But the image vanishes, and I lie blinking at the sky. Dazed. Collapsed. Defeated.

Slowly I sit up. Take deep breaths. Groaning, I manage to stand and look around. Scarlett is about ten feet away, grazing. I can tell by the tilt of her ears that she's aware of me. At least she hasn't run off. The grass is wet from the rain last night, and my butt is soaked. I look down and find smears of grass and mud. I bend to brush them off and am relieved to realize nothing is broken. At least, not physically.

"Hey. Are you okay?" I look toward the voice and find Deepa jogging toward me.

"Yeah, I think so."

"Phew." She looks me over. "That was quite a fall."

"You saw it? I didn't think anyone else was around."

"I just got here," she says. "And I heard a horse galloping out here so came to see." Her brow is knit with concern. "Are you sure you're all right?"

I sigh. "No doubt I'll have some bruises. But other than that"—I flex my arms and stretch out my back—"I'm fine."

She nods. "Okay. Do you want me to get Scarlett?"

"No thanks. I'll get her."

"Are you going to get back on?" she asks.

I hesitate. That's what they say. If you fall, you need to get right back on. Don't allow room for fear to take hold. "I don't know. I suck at riding. I've been taking lessons, and I'm just getting worse."

Deepa snorts. "Um, yeah. No wonder."

I squint at her. "What do you mean?"

"I mean that Vicki is screwing up. I've watched some of your lessons. She keeps mixing up Western and English aids. Half the time she tells you one thing, and then she tells you the other."

"What?"

"You haven't noticed how she keeps changing what she says about using your reins?" Deepa asks. "Especially about contact with the bit? And how she keeps criticizing Scarlett's head carriage?"

"I thought that was just me getting it wrong."

"No, girl." Deepa shakes her head. "*She's* messing up."

"If that's true," I say slowly, "why would she do that?"

"I don't think she's doing it on purpose. I think she forgets who she's teaching. Goes on autopilot or something. Plus," Deepa adds, "I know she doesn't like Western style."

* * *

Dr. Rosa's office seems smaller. I don't know why. Maybe it's because of all the time I've spent outdoors. I've missed a few appointments, but she's kept calling to remind me. I find her unchanged. Warm, smiling, accepting. Her kindness is a relief, so overwhelming that tears spring to my eyes.

She doesn't comment on the tears I quickly wipe away. She simply goes through her usual check-in questions about food and sleep. I tell her I'm eating well. And the nightmares don't happen every night. Often I'm physically tired enough to fall asleep. Smiling, she asks, "And how is your new horse?"

I take out my phone and show her a picture.

"Oh my!" Dr. Rosa gasps. "What a gorgeous creature."

Beaming, I nod.

"And look at you, smiling." Dr. Rosa shakes her head. "I take it this was a good choice for you?"

My smile fades. "It's been a steep learning curve."

"I can imagine. But you're getting help from the stable, aren't you?"

"Ye-es." I put the phone down. "Sort of."

"Hmm. That sounds rather doubtful." She doesn't say more. She simply looks at me expectantly.

And for once, I talk. And talk. I tell her how much I love being with Scarlett. Love *her*. How she's always present in the moment, and that keeps me there too. But I also tell about the culture of judgment at the stable. About how badly I've done with riding. That I have a new fear—that it will never be about fun. It's hard. And the instructor is making it harder.

She listens quietly, nodding now and then.

I end with a blurt. "I don't know what to do."

Dr. Rosa sighs. "It does sound difficult. But you've shown great determination and courage in taking this on. And what I'm hearing is that you still want this. You want Scarlett in your life."

"Yes. But it's not fair to her. I feel guilty about how confused she must be—about what I'm doing with her. And about how she mostly just stands around in small spaces. Never getting to stretch her legs and run. It seems so unnatural. It's like how I was, stuck in my apartment."

She nods. "She's really helped you out with that."

"Yeah. And what have I done for her?" I ask bitterly.

"Well, what are your options?" she asks. "Can you find another stable?"

"I've thought about it. But the one I'm at is supposed to be the best in the area."

"Best for whom?" she asks.

She has a point. Not for me. Not for Scarlett.

"I'll look into it." I say.

"Good. And Julie?"

Her gentle eyes are watching me.

"Has there been any improvement in your memory?"

I think about that flashback. There was something. But not enough to matter. I shake my head.

Eleven

THE ONLINE HORSE forum has plenty of options for boarding. Blackwood is listed. But one ad stands out:

Natural Horsemanship training for you and your horse. Limited space available. Full herd turnout on thirty-acre property. Miles of nearby trails. Len Lawson has twenty years' experience as a genuine cowboy. Honest evaluations for horse and rider. Learn to build a partnership with your horse. Board price includes training.

It sounds perfect. And expensive. But when I calculate how much I'm paying now for lessons on top of boarding, it's not much more. I click onto the website, and the place looks beautiful. Contented horses are pictured grazing in an open field. The barn is sweet. The images of trails wandering through forest are stunning. Len Lawson's photo shows a grinning man wearing a white shirt and a black cowboy hat. He's sitting atop a fence rail, looking relaxed and friendly.

The only drawback I can see is the distance. It will take forty-five minutes of driving to get there. But if I only went once a day, that could work. And if Scarlett was able to run free in a field, that would be awesome for her.

I read through some online testimonials and decide. This is it. I send an email, asking if there is still an opening. Then I cross my fingers and wait.

The reply comes the next morning. *We have one opening left for July 1. If you want it, come on out and meet us. If we have a mutual understanding, first-month board will secure your spot.*

July 1 is only a week away! I type a quick response. *I'll be there in an hour.* This means missing my morning with Scarlett, but it's worth it. I make toast and coffee to take in the car and go. I remember to stop at the bank and withdraw money. I'm certain this will be right.

And it is. The long gravel driveway is lined with trees. Peaceful horses wander in huge pastures on either side. Scarlett will be so happy here! The barn is small and cute, exactly like the picture. It's painted traditional red with white trim. A modest house with a porch sits on the other side of the barnyard. There aren't any potted flowers around, like at Blackwood. But the rustic feel is charming.

I park and look around. Faint voices come from the barn. I take a deep breath and head through the open door. The interior is cool and dim. "Hello?" I call.

The voices pause, and a door at the other end swings open. Sunlight beams in, silhouetting a tall man in a cowboy hat. "Howdy," he says. "How can I help you?"

Howdy? I suppress a giggle. "I'm Julie. I emailed earlier?"

"Oh, yeah. Well, come on through. I was just finishing up with a horse here. You can watch, if you like." I approach, and he extends a hand. "I'm Len. Pleased to meet you, Julie."

His hand is warm, and large enough to engulf mine. "Um. Thanks. You too." His smile is dazzling, and my hand tingles at his touch. I pull away quickly.

He motions for me to go ahead of him. I sidle past and find the owner of the other voice. A young woman is standing beside a pen built of smooth metal pipes. She's watching a horse inside the pen.

"Riley," Len says, "this is Julie. She's thinking of bringing her horse here."

Riley turns and nods. "Hi." I get a glimpse of red-rimmed eyes, but she quickly turns back to the horse. We join her at the pen, and she rubs her eyes. "Damn allergies."

Len points at the horse. It's saddled, and its neck is stained dark with sweat. "Riley, why don't you get on and walk him around some. Cool him out."

She hesitates, glancing sideways at Len.

"He'll be fine," Len says. "You'll see."

Riley's mouth turns down, but she steps into the pen. It's round, about sixty feet across. The horse continues to stand quietly as Riley approaches. I wonder if I look as uncertain as she does when I go to ride.

She gets on and gathers the reins. Len

watches as Riley and the horse circle the pen. He calls, "Relax. Smile." No criticism.

Riley produces a weak smile. But a moment later it widens. She glances toward us. "Wow. He's being really good."

"Yep. That's what we want, eh? Nice and easy. Good job, Riley. You two will be out on the trails in no time."

She beams, and I say, "That's what I want to do with my horse. Trail riding."

Len looks at me. "That right? Tell me about your horse. Any problems?"

"Not really. I mean, maybe a few. Like, she ran away with me. But I think that was my fault."

He chuckles, a deep, pleasant rumble. "Well, I'm not going to disagree with you." He lays a hand on my shoulder. "In my experience, bad behaviour of the horse is due to bad behaviour of the human."

The skin at the back of my neck prickles.

This man is attractive. And there's something vaguely familiar about him, but I'm certain we've never met. I shift away, and his hand drops.

"How long have you been riding?" he asks.

I tell him. He asks a few more questions about Scarlett and finds out she's only five. "Well now, that's young. But she ought to be okay with some sweaty saddle blankets."

"What?"

The chuckle emerges again. "That means some work. As in, she works up a sweat. Where did you get her?"

"I bought her from Shirley Henderson."

Something flickers in his eyes. "She didn't mention me?"

"Shirley? No. I haven't spoken to her since I bought Scarlett. Why?"

He shrugs. "It's nothing. So, what do you say? You want to bring your horse here?"

I nod. "Yes. I think so. I mean, you'll be giving me and Scarlett lessons, right?" I point to Riley. "And then I can go out on the trails?"

"Yup. I can get you there. Although I might want to start off with the horse first. See where she's at."

"What do you mean?" I ask.

"I mean I'll evaluate your horse. Do some groundwork with her. Put some miles on her." He nods toward Riley's horse. "Like this one. I worked him for a couple weeks before Riley came back into the picture. Sound okay to you?"

"Um...I can come and watch, right?"

He grins. "If you can keep up with us on the trails, sure."

"Oh, right. Silly me." Silly me? Where did that come from? I decide to stop talking. I hand Len the board money and wave goodbye to Riley. When I drive away, I'm almost dizzy with excitement. This is where I should have begun. A small place like this with trails and a relaxed atmosphere. I've done the right thing for Scarlett. It's going to be wonderful.

Twelve

I CALL KERRY to tell her about the new stable. And how awkward it was to tell Vicki I was leaving Blackwood. "She was steamed. Told me how she'd bent over backward to help me. I felt like a kid in the principal's office."

Kerry laughs. "I get that. We were called in there a time or two. Remember when we posted the video of that jock, Nick, when he was bullying Aram? His face looked so vile and nasty. What was that hashtag you used?"

"Ugly goes right to the bone. He was such a scuzz-ball."

"You never could stand bullies," Kerry says.

"Yeah." Something about the turn in the conversation bothers me. "Anyway, I was supposed to give Vicki a month's notice. I had to pay her too for the month of July."

"Wow. Expensive."

"It's worth it," I reply. "I can't wait to get Scarlett out of there."

I find a horse hauler for hire through the online forum and pass the week packing up Scarlett's tack. Leading her on long walks to patches of grass. Dreaming of the day we'll be traveling trails through forest and meadow.

Deepa is the only one at Blackwood who will talk to me. She listens to my description of the new barn and smiles. "It sounds nice, Julie. I hope it works out."

It will. When the horse hauler arrives to load Scarlett on the trailer, all goes well. I follow behind with her tack in my car. The drive seems to take forever, but at last we're pulling up in front of the cute barn.

Len emerges from the small house and strides toward us. "Howdy."

"Hey," I say. I feel oddly shy and turn to watch the hauler opening the trailer door.

Scarlett emerges, backing out fast.

"Whoa there," Len barks.

Scarlett stops. Like before, when she arrived at Blackwood, she raises her head high to gaze around. She swings her head from side to side, pulling on the lead rope. I go toward her, murmuring, "Easy, girl."

Len gets there first. He takes the lead line from the hauler and jerks on it, hard. Scarlett snorts, her body tense, and looks at him. "That's right," Len says. "You better pay attention."

But she goes to swing her head past him, and his arm shoots out, blocking her. "Damn. Some bad habits here." He jerks on the line again, then flaps his arms at her. The line snakes up and down between him and Scarlett. She backs away.

Len looks at me. "She's got no respect for personal space. But don't worry. We can fix that." He quits flapping the line, and Scarlett stops backing up. Then she starts forward, and he snaps the line again. She stops. He eyes her and says, "Looks like she learns fast."

I let out a breath I didn't know I was holding. "Shirley said she's got a good mind."

"Yeah? Let's hope she's right about that. I'll give you my honest opinion once we get better acquainted."

I flush. Getting acquainted wasn't something I'd considered. The idea is uncomfortable.

"Me and your horse." Len is grinning at me as if he knows what I'm thinking.

"Oh. Right. Ha-ha." Oh my god. Could his eyes be any bluer? I look away and find the hauler waiting beside the trailer. To her I say, "Thanks so much."

"No problem. Let me know if you need another haul sometime." She lifts a hand and climbs into the cab of her truck.

I wave back and glance at Len. "So. I've got Scarlett's tack in my car. Is there a place I can put it?"

"Sure is. But first let's get your horse put away." He starts leading her toward a pasture gate.

I follow. "You're putting her out there already?"

"Yup."

Scarlett is clearly eager to reach the pasture. Her neck is arched, and her ears tilt forward. But she doesn't pull on the line or try to charge ahead of Len the way she started doing with me. I can already see a difference. He reaches the gate, and she stands still, muscles taut. He waits a moment, then opens it and leads her through. She rushes forward, straining the line. He leads her right back out again.

"You're not letting her go?" I ask.

"Only when she's ready to stand quietly while I take off the halter. Hold on to her for a minute."

He hands me the line and walks away. Now what? I wait with Scarlett, and she starts eating the grass along the fence line. I follow along with her. Every few minutes she raises her head and gazes longingly at the horses in the distance.

When Len returns, he's carrying a rope halter with a much longer lead line. "What are you doing over there?" he asks.

We've wandered some distance. I tug

repeatedly on Scarlett's lead rope and finally get her moving back to the gate.

Len shakes his head. "I can see where some of her respect issues come from. Horse ought to listen the first time. And be able to stand without eating for a few minutes."

"I just wanted to keep her calm. Grazing helps."

"So does discipline," he says. He loops the long line he carries around her neck, then switches her green halter for the rope one. "Now watch."

He leads Scarlett through the gate again, and once more she strains to be freed. Len yanks hard on the line, then starts swinging the long end toward her. I gasp as it snaps into her face, and Scarlett backs away fast. He stops swinging and pulls her toward him. Then he waits. Again Scarlett tries to leave. And again the swinging rope snakes out. Over and over, Len brings her toward him and then sends her backward by shaking the rope. There's domination in the way he stands. My palms are sweating.

At last he decides she's ready and releases her. She continues to stand in front of him. "All right," he says. He turns his back to her and comes through the gate.

I keep my eyes on Scarlett. It takes a few seconds before she realizes she's free to go. She wanders a few steps, drops her head to graze. Then she lifts her head, and without looking back, she trots toward the horses in the distance.

A fist of anxiety closes around my heart. It feels like I just lost her.

Thirteen

I HATE HEARING the quaver in my voice as I ask, "Will she be all right?"

Len is already walking away. Over his shoulder he says, "Should be fine. Old Brown Betty is the boss mare, and she'll sort it out."

"But..." I keep my gaze glued to Scarlett. She's almost reached the herd, and some of the other horses are reacting. Their heads come up, and a few of them move toward her.

A voice calls from the house porch. "Dad? It's time to go." I glance over and see a boy clad in jeans and a T-shirt. Dad? I don't know why, but there's relief in knowing Len has a child.

"Be right there," Len yells. He looks back at me. "Come on. I'll show you where to stow your tack."

I'm torn. I don't want to tell him I can't do that now. I want to watch over Scarlett. But he's still walking toward the barn. I cast one more look at the horses, then follow.

He shows me a small tack room just inside the barn door. "Grab a spot anywhere."

I hover in the doorway and squint at the room stuffed full of tack. "Um. Where?"

He pulls a saddle from a rack and dumps it in a corner. He slaps a hand on the now empty rack. "There."

"Okay."

"But then again," he says, "you won't

need your saddle for a couple of weeks. I'll use mine to ride."

"Oh. Do you think it'll fit Scarlett?"

He shrugs. "It'll fit *me*." At my look he adds, "Don't worry. I've got all kinds of pads if I need 'em to fix the fit."

"Da-ad!" the boy calls again.

Len grimaces. "All right. Gotta go get my kid back to his mom. Guess I'll see you in, let's say, two weeks?"

"What?"

He squints at me. "We talked about that, Julie. I'll start out with your horse. Then we'll get to you."

I open my mouth to say I'll still be visiting, but again he's walking away. He climbs into a black pickup truck, and the boy joins him. They drive away, and in the sudden silence I hear a horse squealing.

Scarlett! I run for the pasture, duck through the fence and race toward the horses.

Several of them are milling around. One swings her rump toward Scarlett as she does the same. They kick out at each other, and there's more squealing.

My chest pounds as I get closer, and my brain screams questions. How can I break up a horse fight? What if she's hurt? Why didn't I bring a halter? What can I do?

At my approach, some of the horses scatter. There's about eight of them, and it seems the fight is only between Scarlett and a brown mare. "Stop it!" I yell.

They ignore me. Again they squeal and kick at each other. I'm close enough now to see they aren't connecting. But they could. And then they do. The brown mare's hoof grazes Scarlett's butt, and just like that, Scarlett trots away. She shakes her head and tosses it, but then she stops. And drops her nose to the grass.

"Scarlett?" I murmur. "Are you okay?"

An ear tips my way for a moment, then swiftly tilts back toward the brown mare. Scarlett is facing away from her opponent, but she's still watching her. She snorts, snatches up a mouthful of grass and walks farther away. I look at the brown mare. Brown Betty? She isn't going after Scarlett. She's returned to grazing calmly. Huh. The boss mare. I like her.

I circle behind Scarlett and study her rump. Her normally smooth coat is ruffled in a couple of spots. But there's no obvious wound. Phew. I move to her side and run a hand along her neck. "I don't care what he says. I'll be back tomorrow. And every day."

And I am. I don't see much of Len—at least, not to talk to. He smiles lazily in passing and says everything's going fine. I can tell by the saddle marks on Scarlett's back that he's been riding, but I never witness it. He must go early in the morning or later in the evening.

July has been hot, so that makes sense.

But something in me is uneasy. After a few days, Scarlett is different. The most obvious change is how hard it is to catch her in the pasture. She doesn't come when I call. Maybe it's just because she's enjoying her freedom to roam? I recall Shirley saying Scarlett had been kept out in a herd. She never mentioned her being difficult to catch. And there's something else that's harder to put my finger on. It's as if Scarlett's on extra-high alert. Wary. When she finally allows me to slip the halter on, she flinches at the touch of my hands. She never did before. I groom her, check every inch of her body for marks, but find nothing. Physically, she seems fine.

When the two weeks is almost up, she changes again. It's as if she's switched from hyperaware to dull. The light in her eyes has dimmed, and she barely reacts to my presence. She still avoids being caught, but her efforts seem half-hearted. When I brush her nose, she no longer softens with bliss. She's indifferent to being scratched in her favorite spot on her chest. It's like her spirit has fled.

It's eerily familiar.

I find Len stacking hay in the barn and gather my courage to say, "Something is wrong with Scarlett."

He climbs down from the loft and tilts his hat back to wipe his brow. "What makes you think that?"

"She's not herself. She's too quiet."

He grins. "You mean she's minding her manners?"

"No." My palms start sweating. "It's not that. It's like she has no energy."

"Well"—his blue eyes are amused—"it's been hotter than hades. Horses slow down in the heat, you know."

"Yes." I hate the way he makes me feel. Like I'm some silly girl. I can't hold his gaze, and I look away. I do manage to mutter, "This is different."

"Is she grazing like usual?" he asks.

I nod.

"Any cuts or scrapes or the like?"

I shake my head. Maybe I should feel pleased that he seems to be taking me seriously. But I'm not. "I don't think it's physical. It's more...mental."

He laughs. "Well, Julie, that's exactly what we wanted. Your little mare had some bad habits forming. She thought she was in charge. But she thought wrong, and that's been corrected. Horses need to be respectful."

He's right. I know it's dangerous to have an unruly horse. They're too strong and large to be allowed to do as they please around people. And yet...

"I can see you've got some questions. But I'm more for doing over talking. Tell you what. I'd say she's ready to get back to work with you. Why don't you come out tomorrow around ten, and we'll get started?"

Fourteen

IT'S BLACK NIGHT. *I'm stumbling through an abandoned city, gasping for breath, but I must keep going. Because whenever I look back, the dark figure that stalks me is closer. He walks while I run until my lungs burn. On and on, heart pounding, legs of sand so heavy I can't force another step. Finally, I make it to my childhood home. I'll be safe there. I run inside, lock the door, flee to the farthest room. I reach the wall, turn, and he's right there, arms snaking out to—*

I awake, panting, drenched in sweat. My hand shakes as I reach for the water glass on my nightstand. It's been a while since I've had a nightmare as bad as this one. When my heartbeat slows, I get up and walk. My legs wobble, but there's no way I can go back to sleep anytime soon. I wander the condo, picking things up, putting them down.

Finally I pick up my phone and scroll through photos of Scarlett. Tears well as I look at her. She's so beautiful. I send a favorite to my mother. On impulse, I send one to Shirley too. Eventually I get back into bed. I lie there for a long time, afraid to sleep. Asking the same old questions. Why? Why *these* nightmares? If they're PTSD flashbacks, shouldn't they be about the car accident? *That* was the trauma. It makes no sense.

As always, there's no answer. I use the techniques Dr. Rosa taught me. Deep breaths.

Focus on good memories. Days at the beach with friends. Dancing at a club. Singing in the high-school musical. Think about something I enjoy now. Scarlett. In a matter of hours, I'll be riding her again. I imagine us wandering a leafy green trail. It smells of earth and cedar. We come to a stream in the forest and the sound of flowing water is soothing...

The alarm awakens me. I'm groggy, but a shower and coffee work their magic. By the time I'm on the road, butterflies of anticipation crowd my stomach. I plan to ignore the mixed feelings I have about Len. This is about me and Scarlett. Soon, very soon, I won't need any more coaching. I don't need to be an expert rider to have fun. I just need to be as good as I was as a teen. I suspect the only real difference is confidence. As a teen, I had plenty. I'm going to get that back.

It's before ten when I reach the barn. As I drive by the pasture, I look for Scarlett.

She's not with the herd. Seconds later I see why. Len already has her out at the hitching rail. He's getting her saddled. I wanted to do that.

"Never mind, Julie," I mutter to myself. My phone chimes a text notification, and I decide to take a moment and read it. Although it's probably my mother, telling me again that it'll cost a fortune to move a horse across the country. She doesn't get Scarlett at all.

But the message is from Shirley. *Thanks. Red looks good. Hope it's going well.*

I'll reply later. Because now...

The butterflies flutter as I step out of the car and approach Scarlett. And Len.

"Morning, Julie," he says.

"Good morning." I stop at Scarlett's head and reach out to stroke her nose. She doesn't show any sign of noticing. Sighing, I look at the battered saddle Len is cinching tight. "Um...that's not my saddle."

"Nope. This here's an old one I keep around for training."

"Oh." The butterflies fall into a clump. "But I thought I was going to start riding today."

He grins. "You will. But first I want to show you something. Let's head into the round pen." He unties Scarlett and hands me the lead line.

I follow Len through the barn and into the round pen. Scarlett comes quietly. When we reach the center of the pen, she stands unmoving. A lot like Riley's horse did the first day I came. Funny, I haven't seen Riley around.

Len takes a coiled length of rope from the saddle horn and says, "Okay, Julie. You go wait outside there. Going to give you a little demonstration."

I don't want a demonstration, but I do as

he asked. Or, rather, told. *It's fine. Be patient. You're almost there.*

Len uncoils the rope as he speaks. "Now, like I said, I'm not long on talk. Better to show you. See, horses are flight animals. It's in their nature to run away. Escape. They operate on instinct, right?"

"I guess."

"We need to teach 'em they can't operate on instinct. Because us humans are their natural enemy. They're prey, and we're predators. Notice we have our eyes in the front of our heads. Just like lions and wolves."

I dislike the thought of being a predator. I don't feel like one.

Len stoops and ties the end of his long rope around one of Scarlett's front legs, near the hoof.

"What are you—" I begin.

He cuts me off. "Just watch. See, in order for the horse to learn who's in charge and *listen*, they've got to understand a thing or two."

It feels like he's saying *I* need to listen. My palms start sweating.

Len loops the long rope around the saddle horn—the same one tied to Scarlett—and stands back. He has that rope in one hand, her lead line in the other. He tugs on the long rope and pulls her foot off the ground. All the way up to her belly. Scarlett tries to hop forward on three legs. She staggers and stops with her free front leg extended in front. It looks like she's bowing.

"No," I yelp. "Stop it!"

Len ignores me. "We've already done this once. Didn't hurt her none. See, your mare had the idea she was in charge. I'm going to show you how I convinced her otherwise. Made her submit."

He pulls on the line again. Scarlett fights it. She leaps straight up, and the rope burns through Len's hands. She plunges, three-legged, around the pen. He swears at her and reels the rope back until it's taut again.

"Still resisting, eh?" There's a look on his face...I've seen it before. A sneering, gloating smear of power. My heart drums. "Well, we're going to fix that." He yanks on the rope, and Scarlett drops like she's been shot. Len closes in fast, circles behind her and shoves her head to the ground. "Lie down!"

Scarlett lies there, groaning. It's an awful, heaving sound. Len straddles her neck. Her nostrils flutter, and her flanks heave up and down with each labored breath.

Somewhere, someone is screaming.

She raises her head, and his fist slams into her cheek. She flattens. And the world shatters.

Fifteen

FIST. SLAMMING. INTO. Her. Face.

My.

Face.

It's all there now, in one vast moment. The accident. Roger. He took his eyes off the road to punch me. The scene in the pen is overlaid with the scene in my memory. His face was ugly with that sneer. He punched me so hard I felt my jaw snap. And then the car crashed, taking me to oblivion.

My vision narrows, and everything

tunnels into a point of blackout.

Hitting the ground jolts me. Not enough to stop my whimpering. But enough that I see myself shaking my head. Getting up on my knees. Clutching the rail in front of me, pulling myself up. Grabbing the rake leaning there. Flinging open the gate.

I see myself advance on Len, brandishing the rake. Hear myself say, "Get. The. Fuck. Off. My. Horse."

"Whoa, Nellie." Len stands. "What the hell's the matter with you? You crazy?"

I see that I jab the rake toward him. "Untie her leg. Now! Do it!"

He raises his hands. "Fine. But put the damn rake down before you hurt your horse."

My voice says, "Before *I* hurt her?"

He doesn't argue. Or maybe he does. I don't know. Inside my head is a roar that threatens to roll over me. Flatten me. But not yet. Not yet. I wait until I see Scarlett is free of the rope and then I hear myself again. "Get out. Leave us alone."

"Suit yourself," Len says. "You want to ruin that animal, I can't help you."

I sense rather than see him go. Then I fling the rake to the edge of the pen and crumble beside Scarlett. I'm inside myself again, tears streaming, as I stroke her cheek. "I'm sorry. I'm sorry. So sorry."

She's still groaning. Or maybe it's me. I can't tell. I do know I can't bear the sight of her lying there like a broken thing. I force myself to my feet and reach for her lead line.

"Can you stand up, girl? Hey? Shhh. Shhh. Come on, sweetie. Please." I keep murmuring, but she doesn't move. Her eyes are closed, and I'd think she was dead if her flanks didn't keep heaving up and down.

I crouch again and stroke her neck. "Scarlett? Red? It's okay now." My voice is high and thin. "Please. Please get up." Long minutes pass. Then her head comes up an inch. "That's it. There you go. Come on." Slowly she raises her head and extends one front leg. Then the other. She pauses and finally hoists herself up.

Relief softens the roar in my head. I run a hand down the leg that was tied. It feels hot where the rope was attached. "Can you walk?" I take a few steps, and she follows. It looks like she's limping, but I'm not certain. I stop and stare at the saddle with loathing. "Let's get this thing off you."

I have a hard time undoing the girth, it's on so tight, but I manage. I dump the saddle in the dirt, then lead Scarlett through the barn and out to my car. I don't see Len anywhere. I reach into the car and grab my phone. It's not hard to find Shirley's number. It *is* hard to get the words out when she answers.

"What are you saying, Julie?" she asks.

I try again.

Some part of me knows I'm not making much sense, but at last she grasps one thing. "Did you say you're at Len Lawson's place? Oh, Lord. I'll be there as soon as I can."

I have no concept of how long it takes for Shirley to get there. It could be a minute. It could be a week. I lead Scarlett to the water trough to drink and then to shade under a tree. I collapse there, holding her lead line, and we simply exist in waiting.

When Shirley pulls into the yard with her truck and trailer, I register that fact. Notice her jump from the cab and hustle toward us. "Sweet Jesus," she says. "What happened?"

She reaches for Scarlett's lead line and looks her over. "Aw, shit. Dead eyes. Her spirit's broke." I feel more than see her eyes move on to me. Her voice is grim as she adds, "And Red's not the only one."

She takes Scarlett away and puts her in the trailer. Then she's in front of me again, taking my arm. "Come on. You too."

I rouse enough to say, "My car."

"You're not driving in your condition. I brought help. Mainly in case I see that bastard Len and decide to take a whip to him." She scans the barnyard. "But I guess he's hiding somewhere."

Shirley points toward her truck. I blink and look in the direction she's pointing. An older man in a golf shirt and shorts waits beside the truck. "This is my husband, Ted. He keeps me in line. If you give him your keys, he'll drive your car home."

I climb to my feet. Wobble toward my car to fetch the keys.

"Wait. One more thing," Shirley says. "You got tack here? 'Cause if you do, we ought to take it now too."

Numbly I nod.

"Okay. Just show us where it is, and we'll get it."

I draw a long, shaky breath and change direction. Shirley and Ted follow me to the tack room. I point out my saddle, brush tote, bridle, halter. I pick up the tote, and they scoop the rest. We load everything into my car, and then Shirley loads me into her truck.

"Now," she says. "You want me to haul her back to Blackwood for you?"

I look at her.

"I guess that's a no." Shirley sighs. "Okay. We'll go back to my place. I've got room for Red until we figure this out."

"Thank you," I mumble.

"Real glad you called me," Shirley replies. Her voice is gruff. She eases the truck into gear and starts driving. After a while she clears her throat and talks. Mostly she talks about Len Lawson. How many horses he's ruined. How he brags big, says the right things about being a trainer. A natural horseman. But that really he's a brute. A throwback to old-school methods of breaking a horse. Known to do awful things, like leaving a horse tied up tight for days. Clobbering them with boards. Roping them and throwing them down.

I moan when she says the last thing, and Shirley notices. "That's what he done to Red? Damn it all to hell! Someone needs to stop that man. It's a rare horse that needs lying down to get through to them. That'd be a horse that attacks. One gone so bad and dangerous, the only other option is shooting 'em."

She goes quiet after that.

Sixteen

DR. ROSA INTRODUCES me to a support group for traumatized women. They come from every background, and our stories are all different. But surviving our traumas is sadly similar. Some women endured abuse at the hands of their partners for years. Others are refugees. For still others, it was a violent assault. All of us suffer our experiences over and over. In our dreams. In reexperiencing flashbacks. In heart-thundering moments when a trigger hits like lightning. The trigger could be a particular smell, a change in weather, a fragment of music. Anything the unconscious mind associates with the trauma.

We have difficulty trusting others—and ourselves. Some are afraid to be alone, while others crave only that. We have problems concentrating or making decisions. Anger issues. Anxiety. Panic attacks. Numbness. Depression. Wishing for eyes in the back of our heads. There's shame. Self-harm. Substance abuse. The list of effects is long. I doubt any one of us has all these effects, but between us we do.

My memory returns in messy chunks. Roger's method of abuse was gaslighting. He made me doubt my own sanity. It was gradual. When I caught him lying, he acted hurt and denied it. Accused me of being abusive. He'd be charming and sweet. Then he'd hide ordinary things, like pots and pans, and tell me I'd done it. That I was stupid. Lucky to have him because no one else would. He said the people at my work were untrustworthy. They didn't like me. I must be mindless to work there. He wouldn't allow me to share any photos of him, saying the online world was dangerous. Full of lies and spies. Best to stay disconnected. Trust only him.

And that day in the car, when I finally realized what was happening, I told him we were done. He exploded in anger. Punched me. Crashed the car. Erased himself.

Kerry sobs when I tell her. "I can't believe Roger did that to *you*, Julie. Of all people. It doesn't make sense."

It doesn't.

My best and my worst therapy is Scarlett. Best because I still really love being with her. Grooming her, smelling her, stroking her peach-soft nose, walking in her silent presence. Worst because of the guilt I carry over what happened to her. About the zombie horse she has become. She's utterly detached from life. There is no play in her, no sweet curiosity. She plods robotically wherever I lead.

Shirley refuses to take back ownership. "I told you, I don't take back messed-up animals. But you can keep her here for as long as you want."

"I don't deserve her."

"Make it so you do," she says.

I stare into Scarlett's dead eyes. "I can never make this up to her."

"You stood up for her when you had to. Give yourself credit for that. And give her time. *Your* time. I can't promise anything, but sometimes they come back. Be patient. It'll do you both some good."

I recall again the Buck Brannaman quote: *The horse is a mirror to your soul. Sometimes you might not like what you see.*

I can guess why Shirley thinks it'll do us both some good.

A month later I fly home to see my family and friends. We cry together. My mother begs me to return permanently, but I tell her I can't leave Scarlett. I do promise to be better about staying in touch. And I am.

Shirley gathers some stories about Len Lawson and posts an online exposé of his practices. She shows it to me, hoping I'll be willing to contribute my story. I see Riley's name included and wish she'd warned me. I should warn others.

I ask Dr. Rosa what she thinks. "Hmm. Writing down a description of a trauma can be helpful. It can reduce the emotional power of the experience. If you want to do it, go ahead."

It takes a while, but I finally write it down and share it. And it does feel like I've taken back some of my power. I ask her why

I would have been attracted to a man like Roger. Why I even felt a confused degree of attraction to Len.

"You've been remembering and learning about yourself, Julie. Why do you think that happened?"

"Because I met Roger right after my previous boyfriend dumped me? When I was lonely, and he seemed so sweet and loving? My self-esteem was low? Even lower when I met Len?"

"I'd say you have your answer. Even the most intelligent, successful women can make that mistake. They date when they're in a vulnerable place. That can make them targets for the type that prey on that."

Six months later I feel ready to take a part-time job. It's at a local legal firm, and the other staff are friendly. Despite that, it isn't easy to make myself go. Not at first. But after a while it gets better. I keep my world small.

Manageable. There's time for the support group, time for evenings out with a new work friend and time for Scarlett.

I continue to see her daily, even if it's just for an hour after work. Shirley puts me to work too, to pay off part of my board. I muck out stalls and haul feed, and my body strengthens. She tells me how working around horses is more than physical—it's mental too. They've evolved with humans and can read our emotions. How the early mistakes I made handling Scarlett had a lot to do with my lack of focus. By spring Shirley decides I should start riding. I argue that Scarlett isn't ready, but she thinks it's worth a try. She gives me zero instruction, but mounts her own horse and follows me out on a trail.

"You know damn well how to ride that horse," she announces afterward. "From now on, you can go on your own. Just stick to a walk, and you'll be fine."

It's true that I know how. I wonder at believing that I didn't. So we go, as often as I can. We walk the trails looping through a nearby park, and sometimes Scarlett's ears perk up. It's only for a second here and there, and then they flop back again. A small sign of awareness, but it happens.

Occasionally Shirley joins us with a horse she's training. I learn even more by watching her ride. She's gentle, but very clear in the directions she gives her horses. Also in the directions she gives to me. "It's time you brought her up to a trot," she says. "Keep things interesting."

"But—"

"No buts. What you want to do is shift your center of balance a little forward. And *think* trot. See if Scarlett can feel your intention."

I do as she says, but Scarlett doesn't respond. It takes a nudge from my heels to get her to trot. She obeys with no sign to show the faster pace has the slightest appeal. When I'm with her on the ground, she continues to be shut down. Every day I murmur, "Please come back."

I could be talking to a stone.

"Time," Shirley says.

Dr. Rosa counsels the same. "The nightmares may never stop completely, Julie. You've had more than one trauma to contend with. Give it time." My nightmares *are* less frequent, but they're fiendishly varied. Often they involve Scarlett being beaten while I'm bound with rope, helpless to stop it.

"Do you believe time heals all wounds?" I ask.

She shakes her head. "Not time alone. It's more about what you *do* with the time. And you're facing your demons, Julie. Doing everything you can to heal."

I hope I am, though none of it's easy. The

return of July heat triggers me, and there are moments when I want to cower in my closet. I stare them down and keep going. Part of the process feels like salvage work, going back to reclaim my identity. A bigger part is about becoming someone new, someone I want to be. Indcpendent, strong, comfortable in my skin.

Dr. Rosa asks, "Does your progress give you hope for Scarlett?"

It does.

Summer passes, folds into fall. The air cools, crisps. Fallen leaves of red and gold carpet the riding trails, crunching under Scarlett's hooves. And she notices. It starts with a breeze that gusts a spinning flock of leaves across our path. Her head comes up, and she snorts.

"Scarlett?"

A listening ear flicks back in my direction.

"Good girl!"

Both ears tilt forward. And stay there. I reach down and stroke her neck. She walks on, and there's an energy in her step I haven't felt for a very long time. I shift my center of balance and think, *Trot!* She springs into the trot, hooves thudding a steady two-beat rhythm, ears eagerly forward.

She's here.

Laughter bubbles up from my heart and out into the clear air. The trail ahead is arrow straight. I lean forward again. "Let's go."

She responds, surging into a smooth canter. I bounce only once before finding the rhythm, and together, we fly.

ACKNOWLEDGMENTS

Research for this story included reading the bleak accounts of women suffering with post-traumatic stress disorder. I've also had the heartbreaking experience of knowing both women and horses who were traumatized by violent ordeals, and I wanted to learn about the ways they might heal. I wish to thank all the women who courageously shared their stories and became anonymous contributors to the creation of my character.

I am also deeply grateful to the early readers of the manuscript who took time to provide me with feedback. My niece, Carlee Anderson, a kind and talented horse trainer, verified the equine aspects. Enmanuella Lowet generously shared invaluable knowledge on therapy. My steadfast critique group, authors Diane Tullson and Shelley Hrdlitschka, gave their support and wise commentary on the story's development. Lastly, I wish to thank Ruth Linka, at Orca Book Publishers, for believing in this book and seeing it through the final polish.

K.L. DENMAN has written many novels for young readers. Whether told seriously or with humor and mystery, her stories have explored friendship, mental illness, family and identity. Many of K.L.'s titles have been listed as "Best Books of the Year," and *Me, Myself and Ike* was a finalist for the Governor General's Literary Award. She lives in Delta, British Columbia.